theWave

HARCOURT BRACE & COMPANY

Orlando Atlanta Austin Boston San Francisco Chicago Dallas New York
Toronto London

the Wave

Adapted from Lafcadio Hearn's Gleanings in Buddha-Fields

by Margaret Hodges / Illustrated by Blair Lent

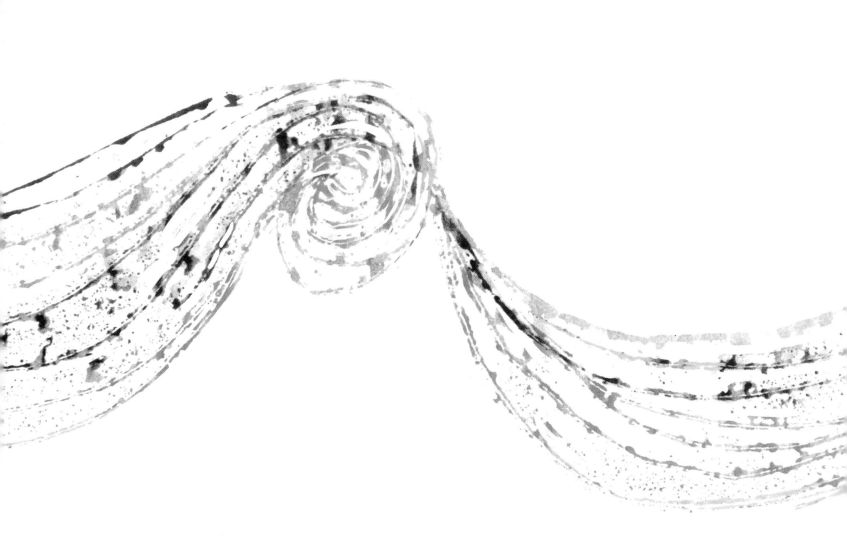

for John and Eleanor

This edition is published by special arrangement with McIntosh and Otis, Inc. and Houghton Mifflin Company.

For permission to reprint copyrighted material, grateful acknowledgment is made to the following sources:

Houghton Mifflin Company: Illustrations by Blair Lent from *The Wave* by Margaret Hodges. Illustrations copyright © 1964 by Blair Lent.

McIntosh & Otis, Inc.: The Wave by Margaret Hodges. Text copyright © 1964 by Margaret Hodges.

Printed in the United States of America

ISBN 0-15-307531-7

8 9 10 025 99

LONG AGO in Japan a village stood beside the sea. When the water was calm, the village children played in the gentle waves, shouting and laughing. But sometimes the sea was angry and waves came tearing up the beach to the very edge of the town. Then everyone, children, fathers and mothers, ran from the shore back to their homes. They shut their doors and waited for the storm to pass and for the sea to grow calm again.

Behind the village there rose a mountain with a zigzag road that climbed up, up through the rice fields. And these rice fields were all the wealth of the people. There they worked hard, drenched by the spring rains that made the mountainside green and beautiful. They toiled up the steep zigzag road in the heat of the summer to care for the rice fields. When the stalks turned gold and dried in the sun, the villagers bent their backs to gather in the heavy harvest, rejoicing that they could eat for another year.

High on the side of the mountain, overlooking the village and the sea, there lived a wise old man, Ojiisan, a name that in Japan means Grandfather. With him lived his little grandson, whose name was Tada.

Tada loved Ojiisan dearly and gave him the obedience due to his great age and great wisdom. Indeed, the old man had the respect of all the villagers. Often they climbed up the long zigzag road to ask him for advice.

12

One day when the air was very hot and still, Ojiisan stood on the balcony of his house and looked at his rice fields. The precious grain was ripe and ready for the harvest. Below he saw the fields of the villagers leading down to the valley like an enormous flight of golden steps.

At the foot of the mountain he saw the village, ninety thatched houses and a temple, stretched along the curve of the bay. There had been a very fine rice crop and the peasants were going to celebrate their harvest by a dance in the court of the temple.

Tada came to stand beside his grandfather. He too looked down the mountain.

They could see strings of paper lanterns festooned between bamboo poles. Above the roofs of the houses festival banners hung motionless in the heavy warm air.

"This is earthquake weather," said Ojiisan.

And presently an earthquake came. It was not strong enough to frighten Tada, for Japan has many earthquakes. But this one was queer — a long, slow shaking, as though it were caused by changes far out at the bottom of the sea. The house rocked gently several times. Then all became still again.

17

As the quaking ceased, Ojiisan's keen old eyes looked at the seashore. The water had darkened quite suddenly. It was drawing back from the village. The thin curve of shore was growing wider and wider. *The sea was running away from the land!*

Ojiisan and Tada saw the tiny figures of villagers around the temple, in the streets, on the shore. Now all were gathering on the beach. As the water drew back, ribbed sand and weed-hung rock were left bare. None of the village people seemed to know what it meant.

But Ojiisan knew. In his lifetime it had never happened before. But he remembered things told him in his childhood by his father's father. He understood what the sea was going to do and he must warn the villagers.

There was no time to send a message down the long mountain road. There was no time to tell the temple priests to sound their big bell. There was no time to stand and think. Ojiisan must act. He said to Tada, "Quick! Light me a torch!"

Tada obeyed at once. He ran into the house and kindled a pine torch. Quickly he gave it to Ojiisan.

The old man hurried out to the fields where his rice stood, ready for the harvest. This was his precious rice, all of his work for the past year, all of his food for the year to come.

He thrust the torch in among the dry stacks and the fire blazed up. The rice burned like tinder. Sparks burst into flame and the flames raced through Ojiisan's fields, turning their gold to black, sending columns of smoke skyward in one enormous cloudy whirl.

Tada was astonished and terrified. He ran after his grandfather, crying, "Ojiisan! why? Ojiisan! why? — why?"

But Ojiisan did not answer. He had no time to explain. He was thinking only of the four hundred lives in peril by the edge of the sea.

For a moment Tada stared wildly at the blazing rice. Then he burst into tears, and ran back to the house, feeling sure that his grandfather had lost his mind.

Ojiisan went on firing stack after stack of rice, till he had reached the end of his fields. Then he threw down his torch and waited.

Down below, the priests in the temple saw the blaze on the mountain and set the big bell booming. The people hurried in from the sands and over the beach and up from the village, like a swarming of ants.

Ojiisan watched them from his burning rice fields and the moments seemed terribly long to him.

"Faster! Run faster!" he said. But the people could not hear him.

27

The sun was going down. The wrinkled bed of the bay and a vast expanse beyond it lay bare, and still the sea was fleeing toward the horizon.

Ojiisan did not have long to wait before the first of the villagers arrived to put out the fire. But the old man held out both arms to stop them.

"Let it burn!" he commanded. "Let it be! I want all the people here. There is a great danger!"

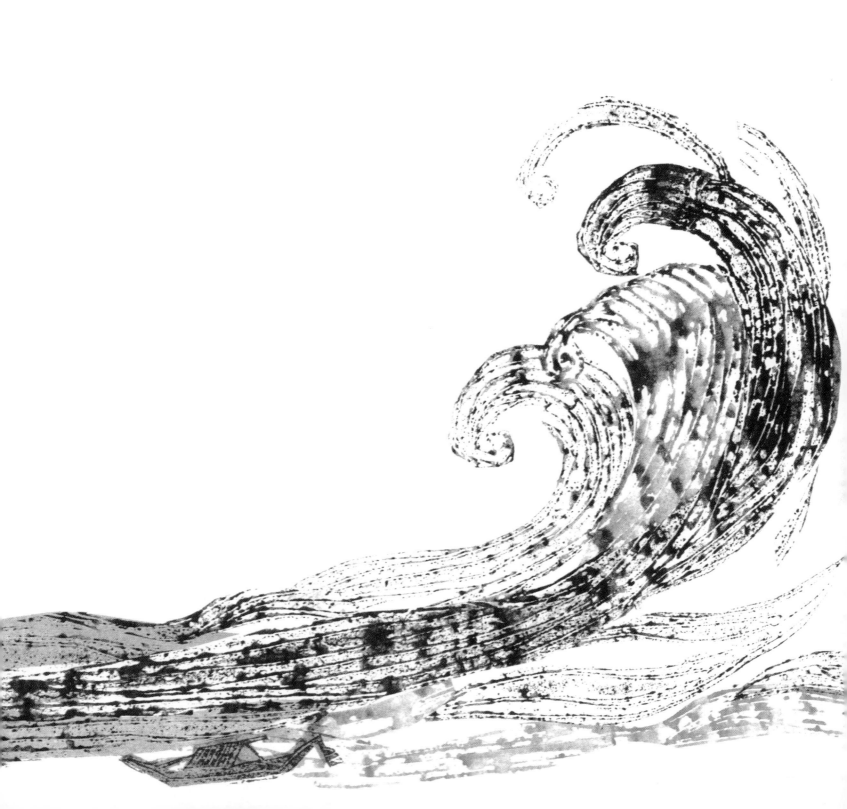

The whole village did come — first the young men and boys, and the women and girls who could run fastest. Then came the older folk and mothers with babies at their backs. The children came, for they could help to pass buckets of water. Even the elders could be seen well on their way up the steep mountainside. But it was too late to save the flaming fields of Ojiisan. All looked in sorrowful wonder at the face of the old man. And the sun went down.

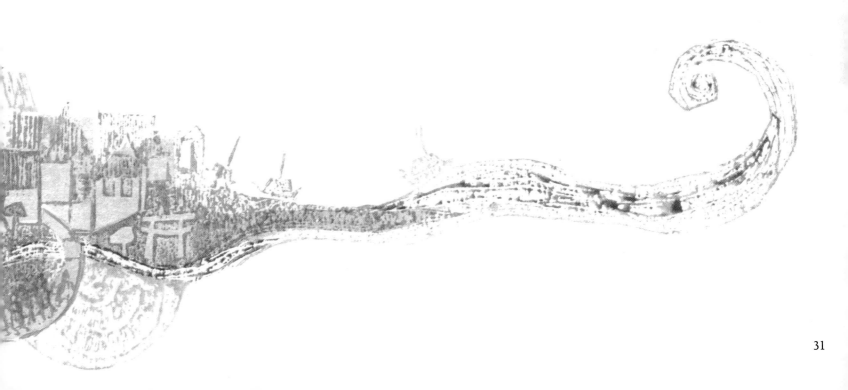

Tada came running from the house. "Grandfather has lost his mind!" he sobbed. "He has gone mad! He set fire to the rice on purpose. I saw him do it!"

"The child tells the truth. I did set fire to the rice," said Ojiisan. ". . . Are all the people here?"

The men were angry. "All are here," they said. They muttered among themselves, "The old man is mad. He will destroy *our* fields next!" And they threatened him with their fists.

Then Ojiisan raised his hand and pointed to the sea. "Look!" he said.

Through the twilight eastward all looked and saw at the edge of the dusky horizon a long dim line like the shadow of a coast where no coast ever was. The line grew wider and darker. It moved toward them. That long darkness was the returning sea, towering like a cliff and coming toward them more swiftly than the kite flies.

"A tidal wave!" shrieked the people. And then all shrieks and all sounds and all power to hear sounds were ended by a shock heavier than any thunder, as the great wave struck the shore with a weight that sent a shudder through the hills.

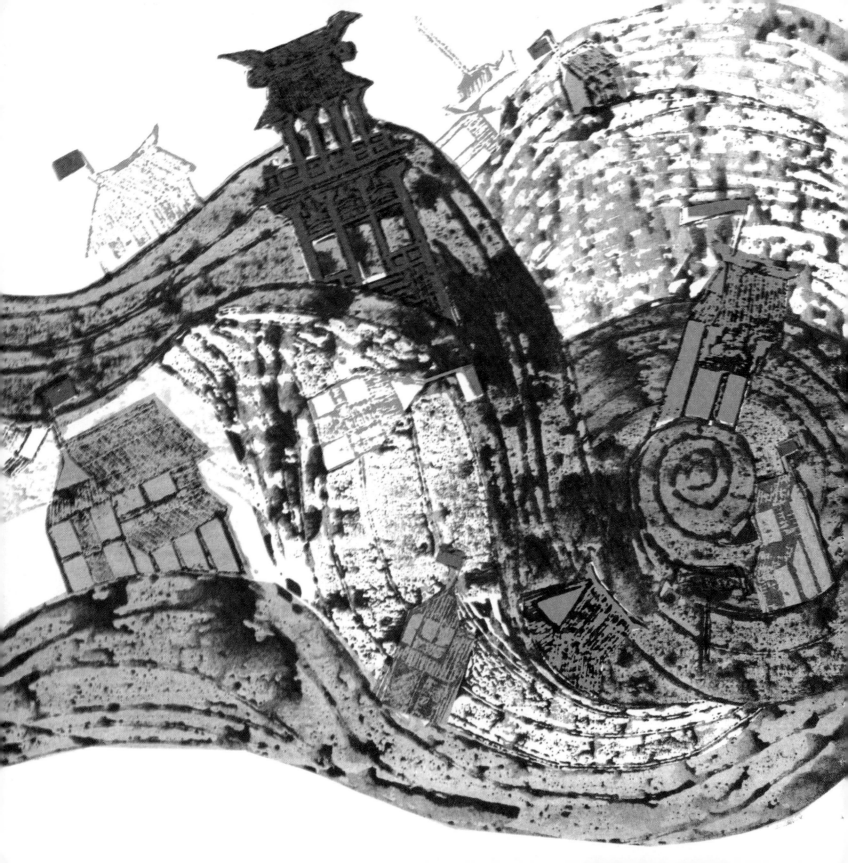

There was a burst of foam like a blaze of sheet lightning. Then for an instant nothing could be seen but a storm of spray rushing up the mountainside while the people scattered in fear.

When they looked again they saw a wild white sea raging over the place where their homes had been. It drew back roaring, and tearing out the land as it went. Twice, thrice, five times the sea struck and ebbed, but each time with less strength. Then it returned to its ancient bed and stayed, still raging, as after a typhoon.

Around the house of Ojiisan no word was spoken. The people stared down

the mountain at the rocks hurled and split by the sea, at the scooped-up sand and wreckage where houses and temple had been.

The village was no longer there, only broken bamboo poles and thatch scattered along the shore. Then the voice of Ojiisan was heard again, saying gently, "That was why I set fire to the rice."

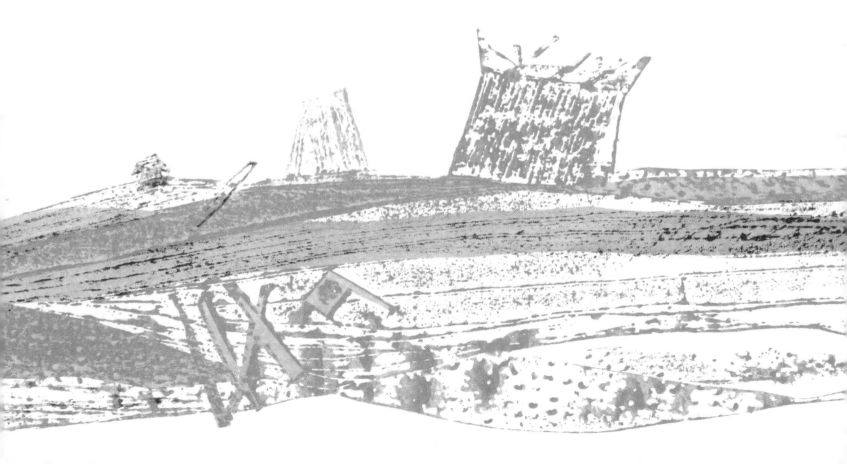

He, their wise old friend, now stood among them almost as poor as the poorest, for his wealth was gone. But he had saved four hundred lives.

Tada ran to him and held his hand. The father of each family knelt before Ojiisan, and all the people after them.

"My home still stands," the old man said. "There is room for many." And he led the way to the house.

When better times came, the people did not forget their debt to Ojiisan. They could never make him rich. But when they rebuilt the village, they built a temple to honor him.

His temple, they tell me, still stands and the people still honor the good old farmer who saved their lives from the great tidal wave by the burning of the rice fields.

NOTE

In the late 19th century, Lafcadio
Hearn, an American journalist and
author, forsook the West to learn
more about Japan. In time, he mar-
ried the daughter of a Samurai, took
a Japanese name, and immersed him-
self completely in the life of the
Japanese people.

One of his many books about the
Orient is *Gleanings in Buddha-Fields*,
Houghton Mifflin Company, 1897,
and included in it is the Japanese
folktale on which *The Wave* is based.
Although Lafcadio Hearn did not
record the story with children in
mind, nor did he give it a title,
Margaret Hodges, children's librarian
and noted storyteller, found that the
tale had all the elements to keep
children on the edge of their chairs.
She has told the story many times
and in the best oral tradition has
made certain adaptations in the
course of the retellings. The present
version, therefore, though it main-
tains the spirit, and even much of
Lafcadio Hearn's language, has been
shaped by the responses of many
young audiences.